ALL LIVES Matter

A Book of Poems

Marvina Sims

authorHOUSE®

AuthorHouse™
1663 Liberty Drive
Bloomington, IN 47403
www.authorhouse.com
Phone: 1 (800) 839-8640

© 2015 Marvina Sims. All rights reserved.

No part of this book may be reproduced, stored in a retrieval system, or transmitted by any means without the written permission of the author.

Published by AuthorHouse   09/09/2015

ISBN: 978-1-5049-2833-5 (sc)
ISBN: 978-1-5049-2832-8 (e)

Print information available on the last page.

Any people depicted in stock imagery provided by Thinkstock are models, and such images are being used for illustrative purposes only.
Certain stock imagery © Thinkstock.

This book is printed on acid-free paper.

Because of the dynamic nature of the Internet, any web addresses or links contained in this book may have changed since publication and may no longer be valid. The views expressed in this work are solely those of the author and do not necessarily reflect the views of the publisher, and the publisher hereby disclaims any responsibility for them.

Contents

Just Like Me 1
These Round Legs 4
Profound Teachers 6
Primary Woman 8
Inner Small Voice 10
Tearlessly Cry 12
Substance's Pet 14
Unhalting the Past 15
Spree 18
Confirmed Fate 21
A Whole in One 23
Common Women 25
Damaged Goods 26
Deemed Deity 28
Domestic Evils 29
Emotional Suicide 31
Hardest Shot 32
I Long to See 33
If Every Man 36
Ignorance Has No Age 37
Genuine Love 38
Less Than, Greater Than, Equal To 39
Grasping at Air 40
More Than That to Me 42
Snatched 44
My Earthly Boy 45
Daily Miracles 46

My Sanity	47
No Earthly Good	48
No Regrets	49
Noose Around the Neck	50
One-Fourth Human	52
Out Loud	54
Powerful Fruit	56
Quite Mundane	57
Re-Lift Me	58
Roused Emotions	59
Mirrored Image	61
Permanently	62
Thin Is In	63
Extremely Torn	64
Godly Before the Name	67
Loves in My Life	68
Truth	69
Press On	70
Peeking Reflection	72
Dangling	75
Hypocritical	76
Typical Day or Naw?	77
Kiss My Aspirations	80
About the Author	81

Just Like Me

Each face I see looks just like me:
Homeless queen, toting bags,
Seeking meals, searching trash.
Some sympathize, feeling sad.
Others point, mock, and laugh,
Thinking, *That's the worst life I never wanna have.*

Each face I see looks just like me:
Pillows made of asphalt and concrete.
Despite my daily begs and pleas
For you to give me your metal monies,
Just walk on by, as I'm invisible to thee.

Each face I see looks just like me:
Extremely narrow in physique,
Two sunken, bony cheeks;
Never ceasing to believe
Just one more hit is all I need.

Each face I see looks just like me:
Handcuffed, anticipating release,
Unfeeling that stealing is really robbery,
Since the victims are actually family.

Each face I see looks just like me:
Targeted and berated by angry police,
Placed in a choke hold as the world can see,
Voicing my fear quite clearly,
Repeatedly stating, *"I can't breathe!"*
But I'm dead by the time I'm released,
Labeling my loves "the bereaved of the deceased."

Each face I see looks just like me:
Bedridden from an incurable disease,
Tubes everywhere, oxygen to breathe,
Embracing much love for family,
Holding on, not wanting to leave,
As life support ends my destiny.

Each face I see looks just like me:
Single mom with five kids,
Often regretting what's been did,
Overwhelmed, eviction notices and piled bills,
Guilt ridden that I chose this life to live,
Yet making do and accepting it is what it is.

Each face I see looks just like me:
Sensitivity I began to lack,
Wondering, did I overreact?
As a matter of fact,
I did indeed snap.
Didn't mean for it all to go down like that.
He hit me too much, so I finally hit back.
Blunt object to throat, I heard it crack.
That scene in my mind I often reenact.

Each face I see looks just like me:
Obama's wife,
Living extravagantly and mighty high,
Brunt of many women's envy and strife.
For most it's an escape into a fantasy life:
To be a woman well known as a powerful man's wife.

These Round Legs

These round legs
Take me everywhere,
'Cept ascending and descending stairs.

These round legs
Never stride as fast as I desire;
Unlike long, slender legs I admire.

These round legs
Can't don skinny jeans and riding boots,
Lacking envious glares and male-approving hoots.

These round legs
Will be so relieved
When muscled legs can finally cease
Staring gratefully to *not* be
Round just like these.

These round legs
Irritably disapprove
Of strange hands touching as they choose,
Voluntarily making me move.

These round legs
Stand, strut, skate, bike dreamily,
Bend, dip, dance seductively,
Jump, jog imaginatively,
Run angrily,
Seek to break free emotionally.

These round legs
Are snatching from me
The appeal I love to feel sexually,
Disallowing my hips to swing liberally,
Swelling deeply in self-pity and jealousy.

These round legs
Function great as two.
One breakdown disables any moves,
Increasing my envy toward muscles like you.

These round legs' purposes are no easy feat,
Not temporarily but permanently,
Multitasking triply,
Functioning as
My legs,
My feet,
And my seat.

Profound Teachers

It may seem insane
To take pleasure in *all* pains,
But the fact of the matter remains.

Profound teachers going by these names:
Hurting and Struggling.
Be it physical or mental suffering,
Humbleness becomes the most valuable gain.

At times more torturous than walking through fire,
Though the Griefology course ends as desired,
Suicidology rears in deceptive attire.

More refresher courses
Schooling skills of humility,
Repressing hatred, as depression thrives on self-pity.

Ego deceived me to believe
Current enrollment is my very own choice.
The master is present during each course,
Thoroughly explaining how pain
Is required to gain
A profound voice.

Completing the test, feeling the score's too low,
Now knowing what I know,
I say, "Discount the failed trial and make it a no-go."
He replies, "Really? Dear student, you're neither dumb nor slow.
How else will I know if the lesson was understood?
Everything you've learned is not just for *your* good
But merely for *my* glory, if you would."

All curricula created in advance,
Prior to now He made all plans.
Since my desire is to ace every exam,
I plead and beg for just one more chance,
Believing I failed due to mistakes and happenstance.
Unbeknownst to me spiritually,
My better fruits are already enhanced.

Primary Woman

I heard a man say, "When I was a child, both of my parents passed."
"Then who was the *primary woman* in your life?" another gentleman asked.
Thought it strange he didn't just say, "Who took care of you?"
Pondering the question thoughtfully, I got what that gentleman knew.
Primary women handle business that most men refuse to.

The color pink cannot exist without the *primary* red one.
Likewise, without a *primary woman* nothing would ever get done.
First up every morning, last lain after the sun has gone.
If you're a mother, been mothered, or ever nurtured someone,
Most days mean handling business with rarely any fun.

A *primary* toils in house cleaning, churching, and appeasing,
Dinner cooking, lovemaking, baby delivering,
Barely resting, then at it again to continue laboring.
Expressions of true value and praise still remain lacking.

Primaries are in tune with loved ones' needs and desires,
But when it comes to what they'd like, others rarely aspire.
Spiritually drained and broken hearted for far too many years,
Scoping reasons to laugh, yet combating the flow of tears.

Whatever a *primary* does benefits an entire household,
Usually for those very ones who only think of their own goals.
Heard it said if you don't work you do not get to eat—
Au contraire; when *primaries* cook, even slack neighbors get treats.

She doesn't need a degree as a lawyer, doctor, or nurse,
When life is the most chaotic the *primary* is the go-to first.
All turn to her when their lives are heading toward the worst.
Leaving her feeling friendless, loneliness being her curse,
Primary used differently is also known as *main*—
The main one depended upon to keep from going insane.
A *primary* prays and makes decisions for the lost souls in life.
Great advice carries accolades while bad ones bring her strife.

It is because of that *primary* that everyone is inwardly contented.
Rub her wrong and it will feel like the wrath of God descended.
Inspiring as Mother Nature, Motherland, and Mother of Invention,
Profoundly empowering lives, as is God's divine intention.

Inner Small Voice

How important is that inner voice
To have made *it* the preferred choice;
Surrounded in perpetual noise,
Inner peace sought for that semi-joy.

Roaring motors on planes flying high,
Blaring train horns rushing by.
Blocked it all out, made a choice
To listen to that inner small voice.

Often professing what we're not sure about,
Seeking such mysteries that we often doubt,
A drowning man could survive through a straw,
Just as life and death succumbs to one law.

Television's bad news voluming,
Car radio near curb, bass booming.
Blocked it all out, made a choice
To listen to that inner small voice.

Desperately seeking what's expected of me,
Learning my purpose takes much strategy.
Is it even possible to be half happy?
About as realistic as a half baby daddy.

Neighbor's dogs barking, running about,
My dogs mimicking inside the house.
Blocked it all out, made a choice
To listen to that inner small voice.

Questioning if life is real or a dream,
Sleeping visuals are factual, it seems.
Distinguishing between surrealism and fake,
The awakened shams sleep, as sleepers feign awake.

Too many screaming at the video game,
Children endlessly yelling my name.
Blocked it all out, made a choice
To listen to that inner small voice.

Most believe we are given a choice,
Refusing to heed that inner small voice.
No need living in extreme misery
When pre-birth forms pre-destiny!

Tearlessly Cry

Just because I stand before you,
Face completely dry,
Does not mean I am feeling-less,
Just that I tearlessly cry.

Aristotle calls it stoicism.
Kierkegaard says it's a label.
But I'd prefer to cry tears
If I am sincerely able.

Though invisible is my heart,
It appears completely battered.
Minute, tiny, little pieces—
Those beats are all so shattered.

Many slices where one heart should be,
As if portions are jumping randomly.
Most feelings are numb,
At least those that won't come;
No longer whole, as a hole is partly developed in me.

I've replayed this moment *way* before now,
Anticipating tears, and don't know how
To display salty liquids in that way,
Despite the numerous times I pray.

As our disconnection is valid proof,
Encouraging all to try something new,
Like watching how I react and act out too—
Shouts are not really what I'm screaming about.

If you'd actually listen to what I say,
Refrain, if you'd please, from asking why.
Look inwardly or clearly through me
Tearlessly I weep, as I silently cry.

Substance's Pet

'Cause I make choices to be true to myself,
I'm pegged as thinking I'm better than everyone else.
Made to feel bad for wanting what's best for me—
That is to be alcohol, smoke, and drug free.
Doing bodily harm? I refuse to agree,
Choosing not to follow, and continuing to lead.
I now find it senseless to seek a temporary fix.
Simply whiffing strong substances make me sick.
Even worse is seeing nicotine dangle from fleshy lips.
But wait! What really makes my heart break
Is that slumped body on concrete in a drunken state,
Or that other one too high to even stand up straight.
Peering, diverse faces appearing like zombies,
Gone through so much, doing what's needed for numbing.
Why can't you see that you're better than that?
No one has to live life like a substance's pet!

Unhalting the Past

Fake it till you make it—
I can relate to it,
Till too unbearable to take it.

Though there are no mistakes,
I despise this feeling of hate,
Rejoicing that it's never too late
To rearrange and make
A much more desirable fate.

Soothing music drowns the anger at heart,
Deters loathing from the start,
Un-halting the past gone thus far.

Soaking tears
Catering fears;
Seconds turn into years.
It's hard *not* to feel
I'm going against mine and God's will.
Is this still keeping it real?

My plan
Is to trade in my hand
While helping loves understand.
Yearned intimacy with a loving,
Knowledgeable, and gentle twin,
Meantime having to contend
With an unwanted specimen.

It's like a pesky fly
Buzzing and won't die.
How and why
Did I
Acquire a life
Of a *big fat lie*!

Actions for self
Unfelt,
Disappointed in all else,
Seeking sincere love where hearts melt.

Love waxed into a robotic habit.
Went from having to have it
To needing to unload excessive baggage.

In dreams, given signs;
Makeshift life no longer mine.
Surreal peace of mind:
Everything aligns
As ordered by the Divine.

Feeling a new life,
Determined to get it right.
Meditate to eliminate hostility plus strife.

How easily traditions can wreck a life,
Like
When a man is arranged to have a wife,
But no one questions why voluntarily
She stumbles upon her own knife.

Spree

Purge: Remove an undesirable *group of people* from a place *abruptly* and *violently*.
  Uninvited babies,
  Unwanted minorities.

Anarchy: Complete *freedom of the individual*, yet a *governmental ideal*.
  An oxymoron for real,
  As *political plans*
  Can *never equal*
  That of a *free man*.

The purge anarchy purifies the poor from population:
Killing sprees via chokeholds, shootings, mutilations.
The movie declares it an *annual* holiday,
Yet obliteration is worldwide *every day*.

In the beginning
Was maiming and killing;
"Newfound fathers' creation" it's really not—
The bow and arrow was *man's* first genuine gunshot

Historically, the wealthy paid to capture and degrade black slaves,
Illiteracy *mandated* so that *ignorance* is saved.
Today, government killings are an undercover democratic state:
Murdering black men who are most likely to be and to continue to educate.

Federal mafia demoralizes deprived minorities with potentialities,
Profiling black boys in high tops, Timberlands, tees—especially
Hoodies—
Accosted for simply talking,
Even street walking.
Transformed into hardcore criminals and accused,
Yet crimes still unproved.

Targeting minorities for centuries is *annoyingly surreal*;
Followed and watched as their skin color makes them most likely to steal.
With black boys and young black men daily being killed,
How can you *not* expect tensions among races to build?

Conspiracy Theory,
Statistical Disparity,
Target Market
Are actually marks targeted.

Bigotry acknowledged via books, websites, even magazines,
Yet powers-that-be ever-pretending solutions remain unseen.

Hunters and gatherers *designed* communities during historical slays,
Viewed and reviewed as a reality show for *entertainment* in modern days.
Lynch, lockdown, institutionalize, shoot, or hang;
The majority consists of minorities regardless of the varying names.

Abolishing the powers-that-be remains a black man's dream for them,
Prevented *only* by extended metal and glass blockades and beefed-up gunmen.

Hostility and hatred turned inwardly,
Looting needed businesses in the community—
Merely a deterrence to execute *every* white male authority.

Why worry about declining food and animals in our land
When the actual extinction is the innocent black man?
Too many officers with a smoking gun in hand
Resembling unhooded modern-day Klansmen.

Spokesperson claiming, "ongoing investigations" to those who lost loves,
Pretending to sympathize when theirs are resting at home as opposed to above.
Too many lives crushed
Due to evil "snuffs."
The real reason murders continue much
Is due to the unwritten rule: *not killing enough*!

Confirmed Fate

I turn to you for confirmation,
Not just simple conversation.
Talk to anyone and they'd agree—
Even if they actually disagree—
What I seek and truly need:
Ears/lips to listen/speak with sincerity,
To feel the same hurt angrily.
Gunmen spraying little bitty babies,
Tsunami gulping villages like a drain degreased,
Bodies never found as they drowned, dissolved at sea.
Loved one stricken by deadly disease: meningitis, cancer, HIV.
Grandmom aging, ailing, and elderly,
Complete strangers handling all her needs
Snatched life's savings due to uncontrollable greed.
Aunt beaten, forced to sell flesh on the streets,
Uncle sneakily fondles his two-year-old niece.
Niece turns teen; a baby is conceived.
Young mom strung out; turns utterly crazy;
Nephew won't cope, labeled utterly lazy.
Cousins feel what you've earned belongs to them:
Your house, your car, your limbs, even your boyfriend.
Friends only take and never want to give:
Makes you have to ask, on what planet do they live?
In-laws and out-laws, one and the same.
Making you regret you even have their name.

Dad walked away, no longer seen;
Totally shunned responsibility.
A son accused of third degree,
A daughter bleeds endlessly.
Evil rapes and mutilates
As death will be the end of her fate.

A Whole in One

Scripture says, "Love thy neighbor as thyself"—
A dreadful command among all else.
Sincere self-love maintains what's best,
Not flinging self-needs aside to rest.

As self-love is removed,
You cease doing as you choose,
Catering to those who choose for you,
It is you in the end that will always lose.

Pleasing those who could care less,
Triggering your mental duress,
Oxygen drained, deflating the chest
Like a severed vein, nothing else left.

Absence of hair, jewelry, and clothes,
All-natural face, plain fingers and toes.
Sincere self-love is felt and goes
Beyond meager possessions, piercing the soul.

To love oneself displays deep care
Migrating within, outward, and elsewhere.
Nothing else like it can compare,
Not even a spouse required to share.

In singleness, totaling a whole in one;
In coupleness divided, half in sum.
Prior to marrying anyone else,
Recite matrimonial vows to thyself.

Common Women

We, as common women,
Have much common ground,
Yet it's quite difficult to be found.

As that jealousy monster roars from the heart,
We verbally strive to gash each other apart.

Remaining friends is a struggle we choose;
Breaking amends, and in the end we lose.

In doctor's office, not sharing a word;
Dropping pin on carpet can be heard.

All waiting to hear results from tests,
Be it pregnancy, gyno, or exams of breasts.

Many of us will dread the doctor's final answer:
I'm sorry, ma'am, but you have breast cancer.

Damaged Goods

Yeah, I know I'm damaged goods;
Branded the bad girl from da hood.
Always being misunderstood,
Would never do right when I knew I should.

Had no *real* reason to live;
Constantly took though taught to give.
My only goals: to steal and drug deal.
Didn't give a flock how it made others feel.

Did jail time; thought my life was through;
Once released, turned prostitute.
Hurts me and my kids, yeah, I know it do,
But what the flock else can I choose?

Only a GED, can't get a job,
No work experience—they won't let me start.
What else is a sista supposed to do?
Me and my kids gotta have food.

Standing on the corner, watching my dad drive by.
I know it was him 'cause we both locked eyes.
Oh my God, how I wanted to cry,
But that would've been my career's suicide.

See, out here I fight to survive;
Murdered a few to stay alive.
My kids live with Ma 'cause I had to hide;
Kids questioning Granny, she covers with lies.
Insult to injury, topping diminishing pride.

A wanted fugitive is like walking dead,
Nowhere comfortable to rest my head,
So I numb myself with crack instead.
From selling to using, oh, this I dread—
Now I'm counting coins as I successfully beg.

Rock bottom for me is when I almost died—
OD'd on crack, attempting suicide.
Awoke in bed, parents at my side—
The look on their faces: "Dear Lord, we tried!"
Drowning in tears as I profusely cry,
God, grant me another chance; this time, no lie!

Deemed Deity

At conception, deemed deity.
Nails pierced palms, sides, and feet.
Humbly you hang, sweat, and bleed,
Dehydrating as fluids deplete.
Offered no water though very thirsty,
Until the ninth hour, no food to eat.
Hunger lingers, pangs increase
As you die excruciatingly.

As others hung near you for many days,
Rome has learned the error of its ways.
Such humiliation reserved for barbarians,
None other shall die as a divine citizen.
Your death scared them all to death
As the moon bled and curtains shred.

Enduring, so man would be free,
Created to praise and not cease.
Yet your desires we fail to meet,
Still you fulfill every one of our needs
According to your riches and glory.

Rising from grave that third day,
Fortunately the law changed a bit too late,
Since you already hung, bled, and died for all of our sakes!

Domestic Evils

If our money is snatched
We'd swiftly react,
Yet we remain in relationships
That steal our joy just like *that*.

It's difficult to recognize emotional abuse,
Especially when the target is *only* you.

His harsh actions to others appear minute,
Like when he monitors your *every* move.

Disruptive turmoil causes emotional sway,
Depression develops as he begs you to stay.

Stuck in a spiraling circle, borderline insane,
Though you desire to leave, you choose to remain.

Believing he's such a good father to the kids,
Desiring to forget the domestic evils he did.

Kicked down the stairs, stabbed in the face,
Yelling, "You are a total disgrace to the human race!"

Slapped across the room,
Across your chest he broke the broom,
Locked outside of your own bedroom.

An elbow into the chest
While looking in your eyes, claiming, "Baby, you're the best."
Wondering what evil act he'll commit next.

Horrible abuse done in front of the kids;
Thinking there has to be a better way to live.

Hope lingers for a better life, if one could.
Even the kids know dad really ain't *all* that good.

Feeling helplessly defiled
As you both know that all the while
You're pregnant with his fourth child.

Emotional Suicide

Emotional suicide
Stems from a tortured soul,
Doesn't matter
How wise, rich, or old.

Emotional suicide—
Tormented by negative thoughts,
Beliefs developing
What's really at heart.

Emotional suicide—
Virus contagious with dark words
Spreading mutating germs,
Not from knowledge
But from what's heard.

Emotional suicide—
Equivalent to mental genocide:
To no one and nowhere to hide.
Though behind an altered facade
Duplicate wounded spirits abide.

Emotional suicide—
Who will it be who is
Wise enough to cease
An endless, emotional disease?
No sense in seeking beyond me.

Hardest Shot

Be angry and sin not.
If you can do something about it,
Then give it all you got.
Not meaning to use your fist
To take your hardest shot,
Those harsh words are spirit killing,
So choose to murder not.

I Long to See

Righteous, hardworking, for family you provide,
The best words of how a great *dad* can be described.
Pleasant moments shared as *father and son*,
So very grateful just to be one.
Those were the greatest ties that bind.
I long to see your eyes just one last time

I enjoyed us working on all those cars,
Teaching me names of funny-looking parts.
Helping you organize business receipts,
Running off slick customers trying to beat.
Some made you feel like your prices weren't right;
Harshly you'd brush them right out of sight.
I long to see your eyes just one last time.

From you I received my very first ride—
That Monte Carlo became the love of my life.
No need to walk, as I desired to drive.
I long to see your eyes just one last time.

Once, driving, you knocked off another's car door.
You said, "Betcha they won't open in traffic no more."
Watching that door skid down the street,
I remember thinking, "Man … my *dad* sho' is mean."
Like nothing had happened, you continued to drive,
That's when I knew you were the coolest *dad* alive.
I long to see your eyes just one last time.

Many thoughts flash down memory lane,
Wishing your life could still remain.
Re-hearing words you once spoke,
In love, you fussed with very few jokes.
In need of direction, so I didn't mind.
I long to see your eyes just one last time.

Final days and treasured moments spent
Wondering where all the precious years went.
Clipping your nails, watching your tender face,
Hoping we could remain forever in this place.
Silently praying, "God, please freeze this time."
Feeling loving gratitude, looking into your eyes.
I long to see your eyes just one last time.

More intense becomes my love,
Hoping you'd get up, so I nudge.
Awaiting response, you don't budge.

Lying there very still,
Leaving me against my will.
Wish I was dreaming, but this is real.
My aching heart trying not to feel.

Realizing this pain needs healing divine:
"Dear God, please ease these hurting times!"
I know, as my *dad*, you were temporarily mine—
Still, I long to see your eyes just one last time.

If Every Man

If every man viewed women as their mother,
Wouldn't have to worry about hurting one another.
If every man viewed women as their blood sister,
Women wouldn't have a reason to yell,
"Hey, watch it, mister!"

Ignorance Has No Age

Unfortunately, ignorance has no age.
Stupidity rears at any phase.

Expected, coming from lips of babes;
Shock ensues for seasoned stage.

Source unlearned, or merely the devil,
Especially from dialogues of the lowest level.

Tasteless jokes leave damage undone.
Cruel comments makes one better than none.

Taming that tongue, not so effective;
Certain mistakes cannot be corrected.

Ignorance: the basis of all verbal hurt.
Best to be silent, as this always works.

Genuine Love

Why do you expect
Me to constantly accept
Your demeaning disrespect?

Perhaps no one has taught you
Those hurtful words you choose
Distress the emotions, too.

When it's mere solace I seek,
God says turn the other cheek—
Much to ask when anguish repeats.

'Bout tired of your sting again,
So when you're sincere to make amends—
Only then—
Will genuine love form true friends.

Less Than, Greater Than, Equal To

You dare consider me "less than,"
Simply 'cause you're a man.

Though a portion of man formed woman,
Every gender is conceived again and again.
A birthing man is a non-circumstance.
Therefore, not a single human
Will ever be "greater than."

It's a biblical fact and not just opinion:
Only over beasts does God give us dominion.

Sounds complicated but not at all hard:
Everything created comes from God.

So, as a reminder from me to you:
We will always be equal to.

Grasping at Air

Sometimes I get so afraid
It'll all be taken away.
Letting go is like grasping at air:
Unseen, but well aware
Your spirit's still there.

Gone like a hologram image faded out,
Your disappearance felt, no doubt;
Memorabilia's scattered throughout.

In parking lot, feeling the wind blow,
Reality check that this time you didn't go.

Back in car, not desiring to shop more,
Un-present to travel store to store.

Life for you was hard to take.
Doing what's needed to tolerate,
Desiring to run far away.
Now I can sincerely relate,
Remaining home for children's sake.

Wise enough to know not to judge,
Effort required for continued love.

Experience vital to better understand
How you ever managed without a man.

Since delving deeper spiritually,
The greatness in you conceived in me.

More Than That to Me

You were a loving woman, yet *way* more than that to me.
We agreed, blood relatives do not mean friends indeed.
Our friendship developed into family,
Helping each other in need,
You boasted of this to me quite frequently.
Hearing this from your lips, my soul delighted sincerely.

You'd always say we never know who we'll need in life,
This is why we gotta treat everybody right.
My favorite thing you'd say: "Love will give you such a thrill, But it ain't gon' pay a damn bill."

What I loved most about you is you kept it "really real,"
Telling folks how you felt and not caring how they'd feel.
Tickled me; you'd fuss a person till you'd run out of breath
Then offer them some "good eating" in a second or less.
This was how you accumulated and kept so many friends:
If you had any foes then something was wrong with *them*.
You meant no one harm, as you simply were "doing you."
It is precisely for this reason your company I'd always choose.

Heart shattered after forty years, fun times ended abruptly.
Emotions are mixed as I secretly wish you'd come back immediately.
I know in my mind it was just time to end your suffering earthly;
I'm relieved your heartaches and pains are erased indefinitely.

Our moments together were extremely amazing!
Reminiscing (old times—good and bad):
We spent numerous years laughing, teasing, eating, gossiping, venting,
TV watching, never pretending, asking (a whole lotta questions),
Suppressing (emotional tears), celebrating (special occasions),
Talking about anything and everything, yet never offending (each other).
Some things we were discussing I won't ever be sharing (with anyone).
Even enjoying, just sitting and doing or saying absolutely nothing.

On earth you were planted as a fleshly rose.
Fully blossomed, uprooted for reasons only God knows.
We've enjoyed great days; unfortunately, they all had to end,
But I anticipate a spiritual life, sharing our love again.
In the meantime, as you're resting, I embrace priceless memories—
You'll need *all* that rest till we rejoice again, *eternally*!

Snatched

I know we all have to die,
Don't know why by suicide.
You've been asked but do not share,
Do you think no one cares
That you suffer much despair?
The Bible says in much wisdom is much grief;
Is that why your preference is to be deceased?
The Word says increased knowledge increases sorrow,
Is that why you chose not to see me tomorrow?
I love you dearly, yet it remains to be seen
Why you'd end your life, barely a teen.
Since the program failed you: suicide prevention,
No longer in sight: your own intention.
Snatched eternally from life: divine intervention.

My Earthly Boy

Heart is heavy upon hearing the news,
Unable to comprehend, emotionally confused.
Devastating moment of massive despair,
Flesh screaming out, great agony to bear.
Crying continually, yet shedding no tears,
Anticipating drought via passing years.
Questioning *God*, asking, "Why me?"
His reply, "Who would you prefer it to be?"
Citing His words to "*Count it all joy*,"
Must oblige, though gone is my earthly boy.
Never dreamt this fate to greet,
Looking about, unable to see,
Talking voice, soundless speech,
Moving about motionlessly,
Un-shutting eyes eluding sleep.
Divine peace: soar higher in *Christ*,
Divine tragedy: evolves a *powerful* life!

Daily Miracles

My miracles occur daily.
Up and moving freely,
Painlessly, this day I see
Breath does not require thinking consciously,
My pillow was not made up of concrete;
Surely this could have been the fate for me.
Sometimes I am in disbelief,
Truly honored, indeed,
All these bestowed upon me.
Few things make me tremendously happy!
More miraculous days filled abundantly!

My Sanity

When did this come to be?
My daily goal is simply
To maintain my sanity.

Born into sin, shaped in iniquity;
It seems the worse of these
To be raised in poverty.

Clothes cleaned weekly,
Whole shoes on my feet,
Plenty food to eat,
Wintry months in balmy heat.

Though fearing nightly
As sleep eludes me,
Yet, fortunately,
Not on concrete.

Those surrounding me—
Insane criminally—
Great difficulty
Remaining neighborly.

Hope it's clear to see,
With much difficulty
My goal daily:
Maintaining sanity.

No Earthly Good

Attempting to expel a myth if I could,
One can be too holy to be any earthly good.
Since we're on this earth living temporarily
Then our only purpose of being is completely heavenly.
We only exist to honor God totally,
Brought here in flesh for a place to dwell spiritually.
Our main goal upon speaking daily
Is to maintain conversations that should be only holy.
So if a need to be earthly good is what you've heard,
Time to revisit that Bible and restudy the Holy Word.

No Regrets

Are you living life with no regrets?
If your loved one died, would you scream,
"No, not yet!"
Or bless yourself 'cause you did your best?
When a loved one passes a part remains,
Making those of us left behind to change.
Like that aunt labeled insane:
Though gone,
Her words linger strong.
Rest in peace,
Your ideals and beliefs
Live on through me.

Noose Around the Neck

Sufferers,
You have to know you're better than *any* precious jewel,
So start loving yourself better than a man
loves his most precious tool.
Being kind to one another is a golden rule.
Here is where most tend to get it confused:
It's *never* okay to be made a fool.

I heard someone say, "They're good
To remain with a partner who treats them so cruel."

Good is actually what it *ain't*.
Abuse shatters the heart and the mentality; it taints.

See, from generation to the next it's what we've gotten used to,
Stuck in what's "norm" keeps us from knowing what to do.

So many different types of abuse,
Perhaps even some you can relate to.

Out of anger a fist, belt, or pencil, is raised
And used to strike a part of the body or face.

Throwing a knife, book, bowl, or shoe,
Though it misses, it was directed at you.

Raising the voice due to a bad day,
Accusing you, as nothing has gone their way.

You're made to feel like you can do *nothing* right.
Hardly ever is anything said that's nice.

Cussed out and called everything but your name;
Constantly feeling worthlessness and shame.

You're told, "just joking," when it's a jab at you,
But it feels like a stab as it cuts right through.

Feeling emotionally and physically entrapped,
Like a caught runaway slave with a noose around the neck.

Overall, if what is said makes you feel unloved,
And your heart is screaming *I've had enough*,

You're tired of the hurt
But want the relationship to work,

Going insane, yet wanting a change,
Let me remind you of what truth remains.

Do not blame yourself; you didn't do this to you.
It'll only get worse to let it continue.

Choosing to remain, the harm will dwell,
Since only your partner can change themself.
You must do as your heart feels compelled.

One-Fourth Human

Don't it make you feel good hearing how pretty you are?
Well, he said the same thang to Vonquisha and Starr.

Though flattered, you still walk with a look of snoot.
Pissed, he retorts, "Yeah, well, puppies are cute too!"
You roll your eyes and walk away.
What you really wanna say,
"Aaah—that's why I didn't stop!
You got me twisted with yo' other *thot*,
Still hung over at the nookie shop!"

"Wrong girl, boo!
I could never want you!
So, bye!"

"Hold on! Before I step let me tell you why.
I seek a bulging imprint, but yours you try to hide.
How would I know if that thang's dead or alive?
Or did it go
Missing because yo'
Pants saggin' too low!

"Lookin' at yo' draws and crack
Gets you no respect.
Ain'tchu gettin' tired of holdin' yo' pants up like that?

"When you let go of your jeans, you open yo' legs real wide.
I guess that works, 'cause at least yo' pants won't slide.

"From a pimp walk into a warped penguin's wobble.
Naw, I take that back. More like yo' crack is suckin' a bottle.

"Even your speech is mumbled and I can barely understand;
Making you sound like you're three-fourths baboon and one-fourth man.

"Now don't get me wrong, as I need you to comprehend:
Nothing's sexier to see on a good-lookin' young man
Than his clothes fitting neat
As he walks along the street—
With clear communication as he hollas at *me*!"

Out Loud

You scream out, "Shut the f--- up!"
Silence ensues, leaving me stuck
Contemplating, "Now what?"

Keep trying to check
Your disrespect,
As too many times I've let
You get away with stuff like that.

It all began secretly at home,
Isolated cases didn't feel much wrong.
Public humiliation didn't take long,
Now the abuse goes on and on.

You say f--- me, and it messes up my head.
Yet when it's said
By me in our bed,
Orgasmic bolt throws us over edge.

Blaming the f-bomb for major confusion—
Is this love or desired illusion?
I know the answer but don't want that to be,
As I want very badly
For you to just love me.

But in its place
You've opted to hate—
What a huge difference from that first date.

Oh, how I desire for us to just go back,
Start all over on that right track.

So I could achieve
The *me* you want me to be:
Just you and me,
Minus the baby.

Oh, wow—
I just said that out loud!

Powerful Fruit

When you got it within yourself,
You don't have to prove it to anyone else.
Powerful fruit radiates itself,
Incapable of being stored on a shelf.
Brag or boast, but why?
No need to;
Spiritual fruits divinely sprout through.

Quite Mundane

Dare not wish away
Humbling pain,
For if a situation stays the same,
What would one stand to gain?
Life would be quite mundane
If nothing ever had to change.
It's outrageously insane
To even pray that life remains
Hypothetically thinking away all pain.
If there was always sunshine, the desire would be more rain.
Then with constant pitter-patter on window panes,
Just end up screaming it away, desiring silence again.
Here is the point, and it is the main:
No matter where in this world's game,
Immorality gives reason to feel shortchanged.
Reacting means being labeled extremely deranged,
It's impossible to take the good for the bad in exchange.
Become much better, and decide to rearrange
The thought process of wanting the same.
Come what may, joy or pain,
A life of mundane would drive anyone insane!

Re-Lift Me

I used to be too proud to ask for help,
I now know I need good help for myself.

So much harder to say, "Can you help me, please?"
'Cause no matter how it comes out, it makes me sound so weak.
I'd rather say, "I got this!" and struggle to achieve;
In the end the only one getting the credit is *me*.

Suddenly life curved into a no-holds-barred boxing match,
On several occasions knocking me flat on my back.
As I'm looking up, that pride is smothering beneath,
Screaming out beyond severe agony:
A powerful, fleshly soul of substance I seek

Questioning, what will it take to sustain me?
Do I not look clueless as to who can help me?
The only powerful soul that could deliver me—
Though I am silent, can you still hear me?
Can you not falter while trying to re-lift me?

Continuously running to all the wrong entities,
Those who can't or won't do a darn thing for me—
All of whom are screaming much louder with even worse pleas!

Roused Emotions

Questionable thoughts rouse emotions,
Be it purely perspective or merely commotion.

We each play a role in society's doom,
But blame God for lives vanishing too soon.

What we don't do or do impacts the next,
Coming full circle describes it best.

To believe we're so sinless
And all others the menace;
Not gazing at self for answers within us.

Why are blacks and Hispanics still minorities?
Census shows Hispanics outweigh society.

How is jealousy really helping you?
Though her body parts are bigger, they're similar, too.

Lusting that one who loves another?
The one you call your best friend's mother.

Hit one pipe, now a sista's hooked?
Perhaps she should've kept hitting those books.

Account lacking leads to selling vaginal honey?
Exchanging drugs and newborns builds money.

Tummy growling? Not enough to eat?
Rob a neighbor instead, and pawn *their* TV.

Why are some still without food to eat?
Government's excuse: Debt's too high, can't afford to feed.
Others respond, well, just legalize weed.
Better yet, take more from the poor.
Emphasize greed.

When the answers to problems don't seem to come,
Luxuries still desired but can't afford none,
Criminals and wrong doers may look like "da bomb"—
Best thing you can do is *not* become one.

Mirrored Image

Flakes spewing down like salt spilling accidentally,
White particles accumulate, creating more boundaries,
Overpowering cities with hordes of bright white stuff,
As if my birth limitations are not restraining enough.

Vehicles stressing to become free,
Partaking in my world, though temporarily.
Silently rejoicing as they've become just like me.
Frustrations dissipate; I smile elatedly.

Same flakes in mirrored image appear falling up
Viciously into a vacuum being sucked.
My limited mentality prefers elements engaged this way,
But I'd miss my snow angel because she too will fly away.

Permanently

The strangeness of a disability:
It strikes with no clue
As to who,
What, or when it will be.
In conception my disability was born with me,
But my daughter's birth: disability free—
For the time being at least.
No one is exempt from a disability completely:
One day you may be walking freely on two feet,
That same day requiring devices for mobility.
I don't get it when a disability is termed "temporary"—
Even though a broken bone may mend in six weeks,
That damage is still felt permanently.

Thin Is In

If thin is in,
Who's benefittin'?
Men, women,
Pharmaceutical drug pins?

Can't be male African Americans,
Since a majority of them
Preference women (thick)
Stretched waaay beyond thin.

Perhaps thin is still in
For the male Caucasian (or not),
Since some of their women
Are of mixed DNA persuasions.

Without seeing skin,
Check her back end.
You'll be wonderin'
African, Asian, Puerto Rican?

Thin appears no longer in,
Especially for those women
Born within interracial Americans.

Extremely Torn

Why is everything looking so bleak?
Stepping out on faith actually,
Feels like people are constantly
Rejecting me.
Tears swelling my chest cavity,
Dispirited emotions linger in every activity.
Expected to love even those who hate me,
Wishing to be, just left be.
Deep misery triggers me
To envy puppies and trees.
Those words of repeat: This is how life's supposed to be.
Then why is it *more* I seek?
Never realizing how the tugging
Is oh, so very draining.
Now I am blaming
The staving
Of a guilty feeling
As my excuse for being;
Displaced but yet remaining.
Or does it actually mean
I'm a soon-to-be replica of my daddy?
Who succeeded, deceptively,
To run away from me
When I was merely
A little bitty baby,
Leaving Mom literally
A single mommy.

Not comprehending Dad's
Actions personally,
But still relating
How leaving
Is tugging at me mentally.
Yearning for a new destiny,
Dreaming of exchanging
A life,
Improving.
Incapable of explaining
To family
That I feel like a prisoner desiring
To be an escapee.
Yeah, I know they are the only ones who love me
Unconditionally,
But since we are totally
Opposites visually,
Holding on, as they're not releasing me spiritually,
There are other places I would much rather be.
People much wiser and richer, indeed,
New thoughts and a different plan.
Does this torture of unbelongingness never end
As other's unlikemindedness shows up over and over again?
Though I've shared with several so-called *humans*—
Who still don't seem to understand—
How deeply I long for like-minded friends.
Straight up fed up with liars

Who, by the way, should also be tired
Of believing that no one else could see
Beyond those same, lame games.
To bash other lost souls
Is actually not my goal,
But the truth gots to get told.
Now that I've gone there,
I'll make this very clear.
Incapable of shunning fear
Makes it easy to remain here.
My mind and heart flew years ago,
Just waiting for flesh to follow.
I am hurtfully and totally worn;
As to which people to trust—still extremely torn.

Godly Before the Name

Unconcerned by names called by many,
As long as it's preceded with godly,
As this is guaranteed to be
Above and beyond mediocrity.

Let's start with the word *crazy*,
A modest name for insanity.
Making someone *godly* crazy,
Even including profanity,
Still rings superiority.

That godly snitch
Who remains in the midst
Stands against wickedness,
Affecting bodies to heal of illnesses.
You get the gist.

Godly evil,
Highly improbable,
Ultimately impossible,
Both on one line, vastly insoluble.

With no godly claim
Altering the game,
Expect total powerlessness
Or a profound, powerful gain!

Loves in My Life

The new loves in my life,
Mr. Read and Mr. Write,
Thoughts take flight
At approximately midnight.

As I toss and turn,
In the mind they churn,
Previously unheard,
A new word is learned.

Rapper I ain't,
But desire to acquaint
Various syllables like paint,
Some dark, bright, and quaint.

Clever and equipped,
Thoughts float like ships.
Many deadly, most quip,
Jotted down, yet stifled at lips.

Truth

What makes *truth* so taboo?
Truth reveals that those who claim love discreetly hate you.
Truth is best swept away and kept behind closed doors,
Simply to avoid
Stirring up other *truthful* words.
Revealing too much
Generates unrighteous stuff.
Speaking what most will only think
Stirs too many nations in a blink.
Let's continue to pretend,
Maintaining those so-called friends.
Some may even be
Our own family.
I say, "Sure, use my energy! Let's hustle and flow!"
Check behind, in disbelief asking,
"Where did everybody go?!"
Apologizing for nothing when it means being free;
Bottled in misery
Feels unhealthy.
Hate is actually unconcealed envy—
Another *truth*
To be hidden from you.

Press On

It is a struggle to smile
When you've been defiled;
It is a struggle to laugh
When you want to cry;
It is a struggle to live
When you'd rather die;
Yet you must press on.

Tragedy hits, you wonder why;
Efforts are rough,
Yet the harder you try;
The truth's tough to take
When you'd prefer a lie;
Truly rough showing love
When hate is nigh;
Yet you must press on.

It is unreal to not shop
When you frivolously buy,
Even harder to cut back
When it is more you vie;
It is easy to not start
When you should at least try;
Yet you must press on.

It is easy to judge
When it is not your life;
It is hard not to envy
Things that look real nice;
Luxurious house, cars, and motorbikes
Require much sacrifice;
Yet you must press on.

The grass is much greener
For a spouse watching singles;
Boy won't marry girl,
Wanting the best of both worlds;
A marriage of pretend
Is to move in;
Yet you must press on.

Loneliness results without true friends;
Among the wrong group, left empty within;
To remain alone
Seems your only means to an end;
Yet you must press on.

Peeking Reflection

There is more to me
Than a reflection that peeks,
Avoiding certain mirrors,
Opposing what I see.
Sometimes too dark,
Other times too pale,
Distracted and annoyed as hell.
Reflection must be due to a curse?
Changing looks from better to worse?

Variety of clothes draped on flesh
Hoping to alter a heap of mess?

Unlike a knife
That could slice
Right
Through that facade.
Oh. My. God.

Is there anyone who enjoys being exposed?
Perhaps those
Who don't actually know
How life really goes.

You see, we fight
So hard to prove what's wrong and what's not right,
But isn't that the same thing;
Another twisted statement with the wrong negation?
But all we need to know is whether it's night or day.
We're expected to either sleep or stay awake,
But that doesn't matter; many are never aware—
I mean awake—
Just gliding through, as it is much easier to fake.

The truth forces us to actually feel;
Much rather avoid it with various pills,
Believing natural and synthetic herbs heal.

To sleep, to wake, to numb severe pain,
Feigning the appearance of being sane,
Impossible remembering your own freaking name.

In a fairer mirror, I just want to kiss it.
Quickly looking away, I try to resist it.
Double take resurfaces,
A changed image,
Ugh! Too many blemishes.
Once taut, young age diminishes.

Yet slightly relieved, having no worries,
Once out of sight, not needing self-glories.

No longer concerned, nor do I care
Seeing another's reflection, trying not to stare,
Appearing quite perfect as more skin they bare.

Glaring back at me,
It's all flaws they see.

My view changes from perfection to invisible flaws,
From thumb-sized mouse with seed-sized claws,
Their look of disgust transformed to awe—
My reflection, a lion with humongous claws.

Dangling

Watched an "itsy bitsy spider climb up" her web today.
I figured, like me, is she heading the wrong way?
She too has decisions to eventually make,
Like how much longer before catching her prey.
Extremely still, lying there in wait,
Looking quite comfortable suspended that way.
I'm on the ground, and my life goes to "cray,"
Yet I feel like a spider dangling all day.
Frightened stiff of making any mistakes,
Mentally, I too merely dangle in place.
Contented, so long it is here I stay,
Agitated and impatient, I hate to wait,
Yet still not sure what direction to take.

Hypocritical

I never asked, "How are you?"
As I really didn't care.
Is not that hypocritical if my heart's not really there?
Now I am much wiser
And constantly concerned;
Love and kindness given freely,
No longer to be earned.

Typical Day or Naw?

See after thanking the almighty, my God.
This is usually how my day starts.
Gotta handle my business so I get into my car.

The day seems typical from what I can tell.
But it takes just one satanic spirit to make it a living hell.
A few minutes ago I was doing quite well.
Then slammed onto the ground, and thrown into a jail cell.

I told that abusive officer I'm epileptic and now I can't hear.
He replies, "Good." But thinking, "I hope you die dear."
I can feel the severe
Damage done to my ear.
I requested an EMS and they were just here.
But why wasn't I transported to get help elsewhere?

Forced against procedure by a terrified, egotistical, white male,
Whose fond thoughts of me lies buried beneath a bottomless well.
I'm an educated, law abiding, yet powerful black female.
Beaten to keep quiet, downward my head is held,
Like a turtle retrieved into its shell.
Perhaps I should feign illiterate like I can't read, write or spell?
Well!
How about I also submit, roll over, fetch, obey, and act happy as hell?

Too many think women are on this earth merely to serve,
Not to be heard.
I hear someone saying, "Oh that's just absurd! Women labor just as hard as men when they work."
Yet, we're still treated like doormats and paid less than what a turd is worth!
Since it's still going on apparently that's what's preferred!

Refusing to bow down and kiss yo' ass.
Now I'm labeled as a black female who's gone completely mad!
All the while at me you continue to laugh.
'Cause I refuse to pretend and grin.

I never claimed holier than thou,
'Cause a saint I aint.
So don't expect me to shut my mouth.
'Cause I just can't.
Especially with so much bull I'm made to acquaint.

Since I refuse to play that submissive game.
It is I, the victim, who still gets the blame,
As if I caused myself to become self-maimed!
I got beat like a dog refusing to be tamed,
By a self-important jerk with a title in front of his name.

It doesn't matter what I choose;
To be compliant or as mouthy as authorities do.
That license to shoot gives permission to cuss, berate, kill and abuse.
And to lock me up for no cause too?
I can hear those modern day Judases saying, "Massa did what he had to do."
Not even considering that the next time it could be *your* loved one, if not *you*.

Sandra Bland rest on,
As the battle to right the wrongs,
Continue going strong.
As *All Lives Matter* includes Black lives, the struggle has lasted too long.

Kiss My Aspirations

If you kiss my aspirations,
What sensations will you get?
Foolishness or wisdom,
Combined with quick wit.

If you kiss my aspirations,
What does my spirit radiate?
That of unconditional love
Or poisoned fear and hate.

If you kiss my aspirations,
What vibes do you receive?
A desire to move higher,
From doctorate to PhD.

If you kiss my aspirations,
What does my character rate?
Simply mediocre,
Or the classy one most hate.

About the Author

Marvina Sims is a freelance writer and poet. She has a degree as a Library Technical Assistant and is a certified Domestic Violence Advocate. She is a member of the Write for Healing and Poets & Writers clubs. At the age of five, Marvina's mother taught her to read the book *Little Red Riding Hood*. Marvina read it so much that she memorized it. This sparked the beginning of her love for the written word. As a youth Marvina was extremely shy yet empathetic. She often felt the emotional state that others experienced, both bad and good. Unable to verbally express her heartfelt emotions, Marvina found relief in writing. Marvina's compassion for people, combined with her passion for writing, helps her to express those emotionally touching moments through poetry. As an adult, Marvina still feels extremely passionate about various topics, which is how *All Lives Matter* was created.

Printed in the United States
By Bookmasters